J 305.8
Kayano
The Ainu : a story of
Japan's original
640068

P9-AGA-262

NOV 2007

AUG 2012

MI OCT 20

RuAp

Preface by David T. Suzuki

Today as more and more of humanity lives in large urban settings, we have become fundamentally disconnected from the natural world. Stores and shops are filled with products ranging from food to clothing, from computers to cars and kitchenware, all made with materials mined or grown in different parts of the world, then manufactured or packaged in still other places. It's as if we are no longer rooted to a place. Nor are we self-sufficient or independent. Our world is formed by experts and a global economy. We worship money and admire those who have accumulated vast quantities of it.

In this human-created world, it is easy to lose sight of a fundamental reality—as biological beings, we remain as dependent on clean air, clean water, clean soil and clean energy for our health and survival as any other living organism.

In this book's stories, the eminent Ainu elder, Kayano Shigeru, recaptures a time and a way of life that no longer exists in our modern, urban lifestyles. Within living memory, Ainu people once lived in an enchanted world filled with gods and spirits. The animals, trees and water dominated Ainu lives, filled their dreams and dictated their behavior. Ainu elders constantly told their children stories that informed them who they were, why they were on earth, and how they must act to keep the world abundant and generous.

These stories allow us to see how much we've changed. They urge us to reconsider our priorities and to ask what life is all about anyway, where our joy and rewards come from, and what we want to leave to our children.

We have much to learn from the stories of a simpler way of life when everything was interconnected—the past, present and future, the fish, trees, birds and mammals, a world in which human beings were deeply embedded and inextricably interlinked. Our future is in jeopardy because we have lost this knowledge.

The Ainu
A Story of Japan's Original People

text by **Kayano Shigeru**   illustrations by **Iijima Shunichi**
preface by **David T. Suzuki**

translated by **Peter Howlett and Richard McNamara**

TUTTLE PUBLISHING
Boston • Rutland, Vermont • Tokyo

I was born and raised in an Ainu village in Hokkaido. Children seem to be the same wherever they are—they just love to play and have fun. We were no exception, and we liked to play in the forests, woods, rivers and fields around our village. In spring, we picked wild flowers in the meadows. In summer, we made huts on the riverbank out of butterbur leaves (a type of herb with large leaves), and played in the river. In autumn, we gathered and ate the fruits of the vines and trees. In winter, we sledded down snow-covered slopes. Every day, we played from dawn till dusk.

In summer we made huts out of butterbur leaves. Resting from time to time, we played on the river-bank all day.

Using stems of *kuttar* (fat, red stalks) we made "deer repellers" and simple flutes.

In spring, we picked *kunaw* flowers (a type of bright yellow flower). We would play with these flowers by picking off the flower heads and sticking them onto the ends of branches. We Ainu love the *kunaw* and the phrase, "It's like a dew-drop from the *kunaw* flower," is used to describe something beautiful.

The mountains in the autumn were a wonderful place to play. We picked wild grapes and mulberries. I often roamed the mountains with my father to search for shitake mushrooms. I also enjoyed going with my father to check his rabbit and weasel traps.

In winter we enjoyed sledding down the snow-covered slopes. Moonlit nights were truly magical, and all the children would gather on the slope to sled until late at night.

Although our play and games were not uniquely Ainu, we were experts at playing with natural things like grass and trees.

3

When I was a child, village children were really tough and daring. Even during the coldest parts of winter, we would only wear one extra layer on top of our summer kimonos and a pair of knitted long underwear, split at the thighs. Sometimes when sledding down a steep slope, our kimonos would flap open. Snow would get into our underwear and when the snow hit out "winnies"—Whoo!—so cold, it took our breath away!

We enjoyed sledding so much that we'd often say to each other, "Just once more!" and we would carry on until our hands and feet were numb with cold, and our little "winnies" felt as if they had shriveled up. Only then would we remember the warmth of our homes, and we would race back, and once our houses came into sight, we could no longer stand the pain and we'd cry all the way to our front doors! On hearing my cries, my mother would rush outside, brush off the snow on my kimono and let me in. Knowing that it would be very painful if I warmed my icy hands over a direct flame, my mother would slip my hands inside her kimono, and warm them between her breasts.

My mother never had the chance to go to school, so she could not read or write. Yet she was truly a warm and kindhearted person. She would often say, "*Ainu neno an Ainu ene-po ne na!*" which means, "Be a human-like human, a person-like person!" In Ainu villages, the word "Ainu" was a very important one. Only well mannered Ainu would be called "Ainu." Those who were lazy for no good reason and did not do their share of the work were not called "Ainu" but rather *wenpe*, a "bad person."

In the middle of my home was a sunken hearth where a fire was always burning. After all our family members had gathered, we would begin our supper.

In those days, our supper was very simple. Usually we had rice mixed with beans, deccan grass or foxtail millet. Yet, as we were starving after a full day of play, this meal seemed like a feast to us and we always ate it with tremendous gusto.

Warmed by the fire, and having eaten our fill, we would become sleepy. Our *huci* (grandmother), *Tekatte,* would then take us to our beds and she would always tell us an *u-e-peker* (Ainu folktale). We would then drift into dreamland and have the most vivid and extraordinary adventures.

Instead of receiving a scolding or stern instructions, my *huci* taught us about the rights and wrongs of human thought and action, and of the gods all around us by telling us *u-e-peker*. My *huci* could not speak Japanese and always spoke in the Ainu language. So through *u-e-peker* and daily conversations with her, I effortlessly learned to speak the Ainu language. She surely gave me a very precious treasure—the Ainu language.

The Sparrow Returns a Kindness

I was a sparrow raised by my sister in the land of the gods above heaven.

Sparrows of my age living in the land of the gods fly down to a village, by the Tokachi River in the land of the Ainu, and each time they bring back two or three big full bags of deccan grass or foxtail millet with them.

Once I asked my sister,

"Can I go with the other sparrows to the land of the Ainu to get deccan grass and foxtail millet too?"

My sister replied,

"We do not belong to the order of beings who are allowed to go down to the land of the Ainu, so I'm really sorry but the answer is 'No!'"

Yet, I thought, someday I shall go. And as each day passed my wish to go grew stronger. Then one day, when my sister just happened to have gone to the mountains to harvest edible wild plants, I overheard some other sparrows making plans to go down to the Ainu village.

"Let me go with you I begged!"

They answered,

"You know, your sister will scold you severely if you come with us, so you had better stay here."

But I persisted, and finally they agreed to let me go along.

From above heaven, the Tokachi River in the land of the Ainu looked a very long way down. Yet, we sparrows were able to fly down to the village next to the river in one swoop.

And there in front of the chief's house we found the young village girls, pestles in hand, pounding deccan grass and foxtail millet in mortars. They were singing as they pounded the grain and it looked as if they were having a fun celebration.

The sparrows which frequently came to this village quickly gathered around the mortars, and they all pounced upon the grains which happened to bounce out.

I joined in and was doing the same, when suddenly a girl came towards us saying,

"I wonder where all these sparrows come from? What a nuisance they are! And look, they come so close to our feet; they do not fear or respect us!"

Saying this, she was just about to chase us away when the chief's incredibly beautiful daughter appeared from within her house,

"Don't be so harsh on these sparrows!" she said. "The little bit that these sparrows eat won't make any difference to us."

She then went to a mortar, put two or three clasped hands-full of deccan grass grain into a basket and scattered it on the ground a short distance away from the girls.

"Come over here sparrows—come and eat your fill!"

She was not only outwardly truly beautiful, but was also an exceptionally kind and tender person. We were overjoyed and ate to our heart's content.

Then gathering the remaining deccan grass grain, we stuffed our bags full and flew back to our home.

That evening my sister returned from the mountains and noticing the full bag of grain asked me,

"What is all this grain doing here?"

I was afraid I would receive an awful scolding, but I answered honestly,

"While you were away, I went with the other sparrows down to the village beside the Tokachi River in the land of the Ainu. The chief's beautiful daughter gave us this deccan grass grain."

Surprisingly, my sister was very pleased,

"How kind of this daughter and how thankful we are," she said.

"You, being a god, must be sure to protect this generous and tender-hearted daughter!"

One day, after several years had passed, I happened to look down at the Ainu village. I noticed the chief and all the villagers were gathered around his house. They were in deep mourning. The chief's beautiful daughter had suddenly died.

So, I decided that with god's help I would look into this matter. I learned that a ferocious monster, who lives in a place much further away than the place where the clouds pierce the land, had fallen in love with this maiden and stolen her soul so as to marry her. I was furious. I could not allow this to happen— such a beautiful and kindhearted maiden to become the wife of such a wretched beast. So immediately I set off for this monster's house located far beyond the place where the clouds pierce the land. After arriving at the monster's house, I alighted on the windowsill and started singing and dancing by swaying from side to side. The monster did not notice me. So, I went inside and perching on its shoulder I continued to sing and dance—swaying from side to side. Eventually the monster noticed me and began laughing so hard that his mouth fell wide open. Just then, the soul of the beautiful girl dropped out of his mouth and rolled across the floor.

Not missing my chance, I swooped down and popped her soul into my mouth and in the same instant flew quickly out of the window. Then, I trampled as strongly as I could on the monster's house until the earth split in half. The totally smashed house with the monster still inside, plunged all the way to the bottom of hell, making a most terrible sound as it fell.

Then I rushed back to the village and perched on the chief's house windowsill. When the people saw me they began whispering among themselves in disdain,

"Where in the world did this sparrow come from? The gall of this bird to alight on the windowsill of a house where so many people are weeping and mourning!"

The chief overhearing this said,

"Don't scorn that sparrow! That sparrow might be a god concerned about my daughter's death."

Hearing the chief's words, I entered the house and flying first to the right seat and then to the left seat, I sang and danced. Then in one quick move, I alit on the dead girl's body. The people gasped and began criticizing me again. But the chief insisted,

"Don't scold this sparrow! As I said before,

it may be a god coming to help my daughter."

Next, with divine help I made the villagers feel compelled to remove the girl's burial garments. After she was disrobed, from head to toe, I rubbed her soul all over her body. As her soul melted, her skin began to regain its color. And when it had completely melted, she fully regained her life.

Once more I prevailed upon the people, this time to give her a drink of hot water. And on doing so, I flew back to my home above heaven. I didn't tell anyone about what I had done, not even my sister!

A few days later, on the windowsill, I found a large wine bowl filled with sake (rice wine), on top of which was a prayer stick. The prayer stick began to speak,

"The chief of a village located on the banks of the Tokachi River, asked me to take this bowl of sake to the god who saved his daughter."

My sister, who knew nothing of this, looked puzzled and said,

"This must be a mistake. We have done nothing of the sort!"

It was then that I told her the whole story and she was overjoyed. She performed *onkami* (a traditional worship), and accepted the sake.

Next, she poured the sake into twelve large sake barrels and placed six at the *ape-etok* (upper or side seat) and six at the lower seat. Then she invited all the gods in the land to our home. All the gods came and praising me for what I had done, they drank the sake and

rejoiced with singing and dancing. This was a truly joyous time.

From then on, we sparrows could go to the land of the Ainu whenever we pleased, to eat to our heart's content. And so it was, our numbers multiplied in the land of the Ainu.

Although we are small creatures, we can at times even bring the dead back to life. So, please don't scold us simply because we eat a small amount of your grain. If we are reprimanded severely, we may band together and all descend upon that particular field to teach you a lesson. If we are left to eat in peace we will try not to always go back to the same field, but go to another.

And as for the chief's beautiful daughter, living in the Ainu village by the Tokachi River, she was married to a most kind-hearted young man, and to this day she always remembers to send us sake and *inaw* (a prayer stick).

And thus spoke one sparrow.

Folktales with heroes and gods, and stories like "The Sparrow Returns a Kindness" taught us morals such as the need to be kind, to remember to give thanks for every good happening and to treat every living thing with respect—even a tiny sparrow could be a helpful god! Such delightful evening tales are part of the very fond memories of my childhood, along with playing outside all day and eating supper with my family around the hearth.

However, I have some very sad memories, too. My father's name is *Arett Ainu*, but he also had another name, Seitaroh, the Japanese name he was forced to use. My father was a very knowledgeable man and he always played an important role in the conducting of Ainu functions and rituals. From about the age of eight, my father took me along to such functions, so I was very fortunate to have been able to see, first-hand, such traditional Ainu functions as festivals and funerals, most of which cannot be seen today. In this practical way, I learned about Ainu customs and ways of thinking from my father.

I said I had a very sad memory—this memory is of my father. One day, a policeman carrying a long shiny sword came to our house, and rattling our ill-fitting wooden door, came inside. He said to my father, "Seitaroh, let's go!"

My father, sitting on the wooden floor and bowing so deeply that his forehead almost touched the floor, said, "Yes, I will go." But then he remained bowed for a long, long time. He was weeping with many big tears falling onto the floor.

Then my father was hauled off to the police station. I ran after him, tears rolling down my cheeks, but the adults stopped me. Looking up, I saw the sunlight reflected in the big teardrops in their eyes. I will never forget this scene.

In the months of September to November my father would go, every evening, to the Saru River to catch salmon so as to provide food for our family and for our elderly neighbors. However, according to the law imposed by the Japanese, the catching of salmon was forbidden. So the policeman had arrested my father for salmon poaching.

Salmon are very important fish for the Ainu, so much so that the Ainu word for salmon, *sipe*, also means "staple food." For years and years, the Ainu had taken freely yet sparingly of salmon until the *wajin* (this is what the Ainu called the Japanese), who are newcomers in historical terms to Hokkaido, came and forbade the catching of salmon. My father's tears that day were tears of mortification at having the Ainu people's god-given rights trampled on.

Before the *wajin* arrived the Ainu in *Ainu Mosir* (the Ainu name for Hokkaido, which means, "a peaceful country where the Ainu dwell") lived in harmony with the land. The men hunted bears in the mountains, seals in the sea and caught salmon in the rivers. The women gathered edible wild plants and mushrooms in the mountains, wove materials on looms and prepared the meals. And the men, women and children together performed Ainu rituals such as *Iomante*, the bear festival.

The Ainu people, and they alone, lived freely in this land of *Ainu Mosir*.

Bear hunting in winter.

Seal hunting in winter.
The seals came from up
north on drifting ice floes.

The Ainu bear festival, a ceremony whereby the soul of the bear is sent back to the land of the gods from where it came.

Picking edible wild plants in spring and wild mushrooms in fall.

Catching of salmon between September and November.

Making *mochi*, pounded rice cakes.

Weaving *atrus* (cloth made from tree bark fiber).

13

However, ever since the arrival of the *wajin*, life for the Ainu people has been one of continual hardship. The *wajin* were interested in the rich natural resources. At first the *wajin* traded rice, tobacco and lacquerware for fish and animal fur that the Ainu had caught. But as soon as they became aware that the Ainu were not used to trading, the *wajin* began to cheat in their counting of goods—for example, for every ten pieces counted they actually got twelve. They also started to break promises that had been made. Then, when the Ainu complained, the *wajin* resorted to threats of violence and even beatings. We also feared for our young maidens because at times the *wajin* would molest young Ainu girls. It was a deplorable situation.

The Ainu did not remain silent to these injustices. Their anger grew and numerous battles were fought between the Ainu and the *wajin*. The skill and strength of the Ainu's bow and arrow, along with their courageous spirit, brought about some victories. In the end, however, the *wajin's* superior weaponry and military strategy made them the victors of these battles.

Once the big island of *Ainu Mosir* came under the control of the *wajin,* Ainu traditions were not understood or respected at all! The Ainu way of living free had come to an end.

The *wajin* arbitrarily imposed new laws during the Meiji Period (1868 to 1912) and practices that were at the very core of Ainu culture became stealing if permission had not been granted. Salmon fishing, collecting firewood, tree felling, building houses and making dugout canoes all became illegal and many Ainu, including my father, were prosecuted for breaking these unjust laws! The Ainu's traditional way of life centered on fishing, hunting and gathering and it was now virtually impossible to carry on doing this. It was also during the early Meiji period that our beautiful island was renamed as Hokkaido. But there was more—there was also forced labor and slavery—my great grandfather, *Tokkaram,* was enslaved by the *wajin*. At the young age of twelve he was taken by force to the town of Akkeshi, 350 kilometers away, in eastern Hokkaido. Being very homesick he dreamed of escaping, but he did not want to be recaptured again, so he thought he would be sent home if he became injured. He could see no other way out and he took the extreme measure of cutting off one of his fingers.

The Ainu caught salmon using their unique harpoon called *marep*.

Now, I would like to tell you about how we lived and what we thought about during my childhood. To do this, let me first tell you about our eating habits.

We Ainu, living in the mountains, used to catch salmon from September to November. During this period, the salmon migrated upstream to spawn, and we would catch them using a unique harpoon. We were always careful not to be excessive in our catch. During September and October, we caught only what we needed for that day. Then in November, we caught salmon in greater numbers to be preserved for eating during the remaining months of the year.

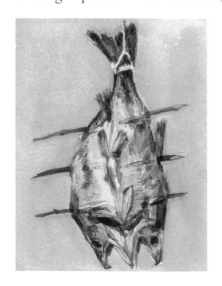

One reason for putting off the big catch until November was partly because the salmon, which had just finished spawning, would have very little fat and so be better for preserving. However, the main reason for this was that catching the salmon after they had spawned would not affect their future numbers. In this way, the Ainu were careful not to decrease the number of salmon and were always concerned about living in harmony with nature.

There are many Ainu rituals to thank the gods for their blessings. One such ritual is the one offering thanks to the gods for the salmon.

After catching the first salmon of the year, my father would perform the Ainu ritual to celebrate this first catch. He would place the salmon on a cutting board at the side seat next to the sunken hearth, with its head facing the fire and its stomach facing the left seat. He would then sit at the right seat and, bowing deeply, would say in Ainu, "Thank you for honoring us with your presence at our home today."

Next, he faced the fire and would pray to the goddess of fire, saying, "Today I caught my first salmon of the year. I hope you are pleased. This salmon is not merely for us humans to eat but is meant to be eaten together with the gods and our children, who are as tiny as bugs. Please watch over us, so that we may catch many more salmon."

After the prayer my father would chop the salmon into blocks and put them into a large pot to be stewed over the fire. Then, when the salmon was cooked, my brother and I would be sent out to invite our elderly neighbors to share in the feast. It was always so enjoyable and satisfying to share with our neighbors and the gods.

My father performing the Ainu ritual to celebrate the first salmon catch of the year.

This salmon stew was made by boiling salmon, potatoes and various types of dried edible wild plants in a big pot over the fire. As winter approached, this stew was especially delicious when the nights began to get cold.

Salmon was also delicious raw or roasted over an open fire on skewers. Raw salmon is called *ruipe*—*ru* means "to melt," *i* means "to eat" (in this case, *i* is pronounced like the "i" in "ink") and *pe* means "thing." So a direct translation of *ruipe* would be "melt-to-eat-thing." This name is used to describe raw salmon because during the catching season, raw salmon is hung outside where it repeatedly freezes and thaws. Then in December, thin, frozen slices of salmon were cut for consumption. These frozen slices, when eaten, quickly melt inside our mouths, so this food is called *ruipe*—"melting food."

We also ate many other types of fish besides salmon. In April and May we caught *supun*, a large red-bellied dace, when they came upstream to spawn. Then in July and August we caught *sakipe*, trout. *Supun* was best when it was minced, bone and all, and then put in a stew. And *sakipe* is a tasty fish both boiled and grilled. For the Ainu, the rivers were like storehouses filled with food.

Pukusa—novice garlic
These can be picked in early spring as soon as the snow melts. They are very delicious, although the after-breath can be a bit unpleasant.

Pukusa-kina—an anamone
Very good as a vinegar dish or in egg soup. When dried it can be used in a dish that is cooked at the table.

Sorma—royal fern
The stems are picked when they are still soft and are preserved by drying.

Kor-koni—butterbur
The butterbur in Hokkaido grow to a height of two meters. They are good cooked with dried fish and they can also be preserved.

We Ainu are often called hunters. However, this was true only up until about the Meiji Period. During my childhood, I didn't know of anyone who was making a living solely by hunting. In my hometown of Nibutani, very rarely did anyone see a bear, and the last bear caught in our area was in 1940, so of course I never ate bear meat during my childhood.

Nevertheless, the mountains were still considered a vital storehouse of food. Plentiful amounts of edible wild plants, mushrooms, and the fruits and nuts of trees could be harvested. When garden vegetables became scarce, these "mountain vegetables" were a very important source of food.

There were rules governing the taking of natural things such as salmon and edible wild plants. When my mother, grandmother and I went to pick mountain vegetables such as butterbur or *pukusa* (a plant with a strong smell of garlic), we never took everything growing in that one spot. If we took everything, root and all, the plant would not survive for future picking. So we were careful not to take too much and upset the balance of nature.

Although we grew vegetables and grains in the fields, the blessings harvested from the sea, rivers and mountains played a very important part in the Ainu diet. Growing vegetables was regarded as only supplementary to hunting, fishing and gathering, and they were grown mainly by women as part of housework. Gathering wild plants was also a job for women and they were freely allowed to gather wild plants in the vicinity of their own village.

1. Everyone would go to the mountains to cut down and haul out trees to use as the posts and beams of the house. Trees such as the Japanese pagoda and Japanese oak were used because they do not rot easily.

2. Using a six *shaku* stick (one *shaku* being thirty cm or twelve inches), the place to bury the posts was determined. Holes were dug and each post was stood upright and buried in the holes. Next, the framework of the house was built by securing the beams to the posts using vey strong grapevines.

We received the blessings of nature not only in the form of food. Up until a short while before I was born, we obtained all the materials needed for building our houses and making our clothes from the mountains themselves.

Let me tell you how a traditional Ainu house was built. Homes were built in places where there was no fear of flooding, in a place that was near a source of drinking water, such as a valley or spring. A traditional Ainu home was built in stages and all the people in the village would help in the building of a new house. At times many helpers, some forty to fifty people, would be working together at the same time and if the building went smoothly, a new house could be finished extremely quickly, sometimes being completed in only two or three days. The house's safe completion would be marked with a ceremony of thanks to the gods and blessings for guests and the new household members.

3. The roof's framework was then assembled on top of the posts and beams. Next, crossbeams for hanging the thatch were tied to the roof's framework, at shank-length intervals.

4. Thatch reaped in the fall was tied to the roof's crossbeams in small bundles.

7. A sunken hearth was built in the middle of the room and a fire was lit in it. Thus, this house's goddess of fire was born. Next, sake and prayer sticks were offered to the gods in a ceremony to thank them for the safe completion of the new house. Mugwort arrows were then fired inside the house into the thatch under-roof so as to satisfy and quieten the spirits of the felled trees. Lastly, dumplings were scattered over the guests and the future inhabitants of this house with the wish that the members of this house will be blessed with food as abundantly as if food fell out of the sky.

5. Thatch made of *cogon* grass (or in some areas, bamboo grass) was used to make the walls. The thatch was tied to the wall's crossbeams using tree fiber (*shina*) rope.

6. To keep the wind and snow out, a dirt-floored entrance was built. The outside of the house was thus complete.

The house I grew up in had some differences from the one in this picture in that it had walls made of boards, glass windows, and a separate room for the kitchen and my parents' bedroom.

However this house plan is still uniquely Ainu and is fascinating. Even though this is a very simple and small house, there are many gods enshrined in it.

A home is the most important place for family life—this was true then and is still true now. The Ainu way of thinking is that this most precious place is always under the protection of various gods. We also strongly believed that our house was under the continuous protection of the various gods.

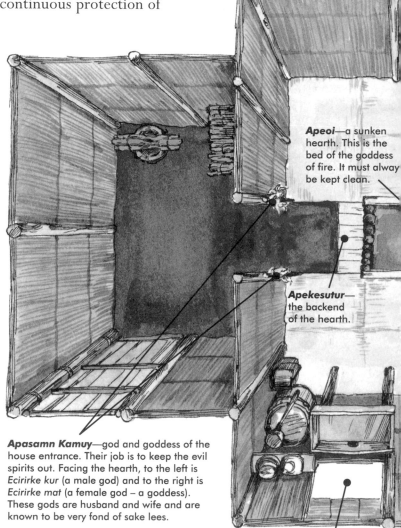

Apeoi—a sunken hearth. This is the bed of the goddess of fire. It must alway be kept clean.

Apekesutur—the backend of the hearth.

Wakka tausi—water hole

Wakkaus Kamuy—god of water. The water barrel in the house was never allowed to sit empty. So, even if it was nighttime we would go to the spring to fetch water. At such times we would say, *"To-wakka mos mos, to-wakka mos mos."* (God of the water, please awaken, god of the water please awaken) so as to awake the god of water.

Apasamn Kamuy—god and goddess of the house entrance. Their job is to keep the evil spirits out. Facing the hearth, to the left is *Ecirirke kur* (a male god) and to the right is *Ecirirke mat* (a female god – a goddess). These gods are husband and wife and are known to be very fond of sake lees.

Nupkikuta puyar—the window out of which used water is to be thrown.

Rukor Kamuy—god of the toilet. In times of danger, this god is the first to come to help. To the left, *menokoru* (women's toilet) and to the right, *okkayor* (men's toilet).

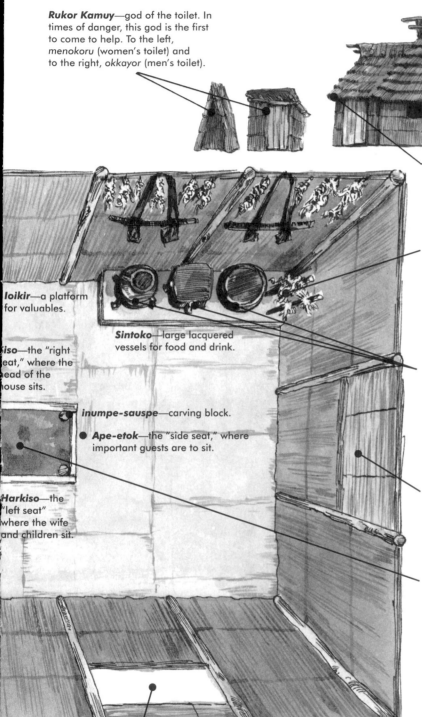

Cisepannokianpa Kamuy; Cisepennokianpa Kamuy—husband and wife gods who also protect the house from earthquakes and all types of weather including typhoons.

Cisekor Kamuy—house god who occupies the east corner and watches over every inch of this house. This god will appear in the dreams of household members to warn and prevent impending dangers. A male god with a great long white beard and is the husband of *Apehuci Kamuy* (the goddess of fire).

Coipep Kamuy—god of vessels. Unusable vessels (damaged or old), are retired with a ceremony of thanks. Saying, "Thank you for being of great use for the Ainu," these vessels are placed on the outside altar along with an offering of deccan grass, foxtail millet and tobacco.

Rorun puyar—the east facing sacred window. This is the window through which a slain bear and ceremonial goods must be brought in and out of the house.

Apehuci Kamuy—goddess of fire. This goddess is usually very gentle and generous. However, if she is made angry she can reduce the house and all the possessions therein to ashes. She wears six layers of kimono tied with a sash on top of which she has six more layers of kimono which are left to flutter freely. *Apehuci Kamuy* is the wife of *Cisekor Kamuy* (the god of the house).

Ioikir—a platform for valuables.

Sintoko—large lacquered vessels for food and drink.

...iso—the "right seat," where the head of the house sits.

inumpe-sauspe—carving block.

Ape-etok—the "side seat," where important guests are to sit.

Harkiso—the "left seat" where the wife and children sit.

Itomun puyar—the window to let light in.

Traditional Ainu *atrus* clothing made from tree bark fibers is well known. *Atrus* fabric is made according to the steps shown here. First, we search the mountains for *atni* trees (a rare type of elm). Sections of bark from these trees are stripped. From this moment, it takes at least two months to weave enough fabric to make one kimono.

1. Between spring and early summer, sections of bark are stripped from *atni* trees in the woods.

3. The bark is softened by soaking in a swamp for about a week.

2. The outer bark is peeled from the inner layer of the bark and is left by the tree. Only the inner layer is brought home.

4. The bark which is to be used as the warp is boiled with wood ash to strengthen the fibers.

My aunt, *Umoshimatte*, worked everyday on weaving *atrus*. The bags and kimonos she made were not so much for our own use, but were instead sold as souvenirs.

5. The soaked and boiled bark is then washed, dried and torn by hand into fine strips. These are twisted and wound into balls.

6. A loom is threaded and *atrus* cloth is woven.

7. Finally, this cloth is tailored into a kimono and Ainu designs are appliqued and embroidered on it.

All Ainu clothing (that is, clothing made of *atrus* and other fibers) is embroidered with Ainu designs. Traditionally, such designs were appliqued and embroidered only on clothes that were worn on formal occasions, such as festivals and weddings, or during religious rituals.

The designs on the bag and clothes shown here are representative of Ainu designs. But you may ask, why do we applique and embroider these designs on our clothes?

Atrus—the name for a kimono made of *atrus* fabric.

Mantari—an apron.

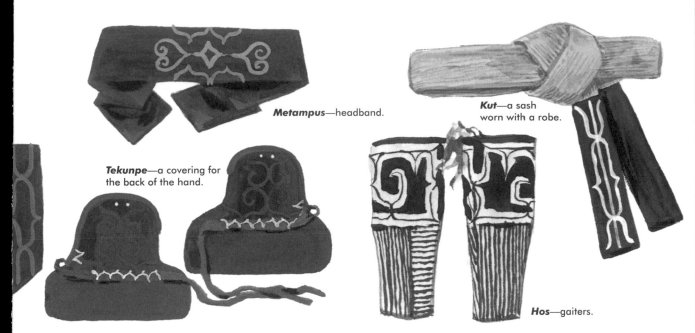

Metampus—headband.

Kut—a sash worn with a robe.

Tekunpe—a covering for the back of the hand.

Hos—gaiters.

When I was a little boy, my mother would often carry my baby brother on her back and take us to the fields to work. When we arrived at the field my mother would spread a straw mat on the footpath and on it she placed a rope in the shape of a circle. Then she would lay my brother down in the middle of this circle to sleep. Once, I asked my mother why she did this and she answered, "This rope protects the baby from any evil spirits that may come by."

On old Ainu clothing, Ainu designs were only embroidered around the edge of the sleeve, the neck band and the hem. Evil spirits were said to be able to enter the body through such places, so the embroidery was like a rope to prevent evil spirits from entering the body.

Konci—headwear/hood. When men were married, triangular tassels were attached to this hood. However, if the man's wife died, these tassels would be removed and would be buried with her.

Karop—a bag for carrying firestone implements.

27

The Two-Headed Bear

My family includes my father and mother, two older brothers, two older sisters and me, a young boy. Just as I was old enough to run around the mountains I heard my father and older brothers talking about the man-eating bear which appears every sixth generation. It was attacking and stealing people from distant villages. No one knew what the bear looked like because no one had lived after seeing it. I didn't like what I heard and decided I would have to go and see for myself. Yet, there was no one who could take me there. One day, when I was thinking how I could get to this place, I heard my sisters making plans to go into the mountains to dig for uba lily bulbs. Nobody noticed that I had hidden my bow and quiver, with poisonous arrows, next to the path leading into the mountains. My sisters started out for the mountains, and quietly, taking my bow and quiver, I followed behind them. My sisters did not realise until we were too deep in the forest, so they agreed to take me along. Further into the mountains, we came to a place where the uba lilies grew thickly. My sisters said, "Now, you stay right here!" and leaving their sacks beside me they started digging for lily bulbs. I thought to myself, "This is my chance!" and I quickly ran further into the mountains, to a big marsh beyond the sight and hearing of my sisters. In the surrounding mud I could see the tracks of a bear.

I advanced cautiously, and there in the middle of the marsh stood two trees, an alder and a swamp ash. The trees seemed as though they were huddled together, arm-in-arm—truly beautiful and standing there, god-like, in the

middle of the marsh. Below their branches I carefully performed a traditional worship and prayed, "Oh, god of the standing trees, I am about to slay a bear. Please stay with me and watch over me." Suddenly, as if the trees had heard, their branches shook.

Walking further into the marsh, I came upon a great white mound, and as I came closer I could see it was a pile of human bones. Some bones were old, weather-beaten and completely white, while others were new and still dripping with blood.

There could be no mistake, this was, the bear's den! As the bear had committed unforgivable acts I decided to slay him. I moved closer to the den's entrance and as something was moving inside, I climbed above the entrance and stomping my feet I cried, "Come on out you beast! What reason do you have to kill so many of my brothers and sisters?" "And you—the many gods of this land, how could you stand by and watch this happen without doing anything about this? I am not prepared to allow it!"

Grinding teeth and thundering sounds of footsteps could be heard inside the den. Footsteps, similar in sound to a bagful of small stones being pounded against the earth, like the sound of pounding straw to make straw mats. I yelled again, "Come on! Come on!" and as if in answer to my yell, the bear came roaring out.

I had never seen such a creature. It was a monster-bear with two heads, one at the front and one at the back. And from both of its foreheads protruded a horn, the size and shape of the shuttle we use to weave *atrus* cloth.

The bear came straight for me. I drew my

bow and fired an arrow but it bounced off! And the way it bounced off was unnatural.

It is said that wise old bears sometimes rub pine-gum all over their bodies then roll in the dirt. Then again, they rub pine-gum all over their bodies and next roll in piles of leaves. By repeating this process, a solid piece of armor is created, so thick and hard, that an arrow cannot pierce it. There is only one place where such a bear can be pierced and that is just under the shoulder joint where the bear cannot make a pine-gum shield.

Having failed to pierce the bear with my first arrow, I ran and fired another arrow at the bear. Everytime the arrows bounced off! Then, just as the bear was about to jump on me, I mustered up my last bit of strength and ran for the nearby alder tree. As I could feel the heat of the beast's breath on my back and my hair being blown apart, I reached the base of the alder tree. Crying out, "God help me!" I reached out for the bottom branch and hooking my leg over it, scrambled onto it. The enraged bear was running so forcefully that he ran past the tree, but then rapidly returned.

Glaring at me up in the tree it raised its head and smashed its horn against the alder tree. Again and again it pounded its horns against the tree trunk. Wood-chips flew everywhere, and in no time the soft alder tree was being carved away and it looked as though the trunk would break at any moment.

I wanted to jump to the swamp ash tree but the bear was shaking the tree so hard I could not. I could now hear the alder tree cracking and if I didn't do something fast, I would become the beast's next meal! So I started to carefully step from the thin alder's branches to the entangled swamp ash tree.

The enraged bear continued to smash its horns against the alder tree making even more wood-chips fly. Thinking this was the end, I closed my eyes and leapt towards the swamp ash's branches but my foot missed the branch, and I almost went tumbling to the ground. Then, just when I could feel the bear's breath on my leg, I managed to hook my other leg over a branch and scrambled up onto it. It was then that the alder tree crashed to the ground. Repeatedly and powerfully the bear smashed its horns against the tree, splitting the trunk and sending wood-chips flying. Having secured my body to the branches, I drew an arrow from the quiver. I shot two arrows, but they both bounced off the bear! The swamp ash tree was quickly being hacked away and was only barely standing.

I only had one arrow left. It is believed that this last arrow contains the spirit of the quiver and is its protector. Such an arrow is never to be removed from the quiver until the most desperate of times.

Putting all my hope and spirit in this last arrow, I placed it in my bow and drew it. Meanwhile the bear was thrashing around at the base of the tree as if it were being swung around at the end of a rope. Taking aim and lining up my bow and arrow with the moving bear, I shot my arrow.

I am now certain that it was only because of god's help that the arrow flew straight and hit the bear just under its shoulder joint and pierced it deeply—so deep that the arrow blades could hardly be seen. Staggering, the bear began to heavily crash into the trunk with even more vigor. Poisoned arrowheads have this effect of giving a last spurt of energy.

Thoughts crossed my mind that the tree may collapse before the poison killed the bear. I cried out with words that I never thought I would say, "Oh, god of the white wireworm! —you who were sent from heaven to protect the marshes, please, please save me. If you desert me now and let me die, it is for sure that the awful stench arising from my corpse will rise up to heaven as a mist and trouble you forever!" Immediately after I spoke these words a puny man wearing a white gown, multi-layered and short-sleeved, appeared from nowhere holding a spear made of mugwort. With this the man lightly pierced the charging bear two or three times. Something strange then happened; the bear began to melt and soon only its white skeleton remained. Once melted, the man immediately disappeared.

I believed the man was the god of the white wireworm. I was filled with awe of this god's strength, felling a ferocious monster-bear with only a mugwort spear. I was also amazed at the power and efficiency of mugwort. Mugwort is reputed to be the first grass to have grown on the earth. It is said that swords and spears made from mugwort have magical powers. Yet, I never imagined its powers would be so great.

By now, the sun was dipping towards the west. I was sure that my sisters would be worrying about me, so I ran back at full speed to the place where they had told me to wait, composing myself as I ran to look as if nothing had happened.

When they saw me they said, "Where have you been? We told you to stay right here! You are always causing us such worry!" While scolding me my sisters heaved their lily bulbs onto their backs and we made off for home.

At home my father and brothers were at their wits' end worrying about where I had got to. My sisters were severely scolded for having taken me with them into the mountains. My father often said that I, being the youngest child, was a gift from the gods and I should not be allowed to wander off too far from home. Another source of great worry was that we had gone into the mountains near to where the monster-bear lived. I went to bed without telling a soul what had happened in the moutains.

Early next morning, just before dawn, my father and older brothers arose and asked me, "Why didn't you tell us what happened yesterday? In our dreams last night the god of the white wireworm reported of your doings." My father scolded and spanked me on my buttocks with a thick wooden fire prong. "If you had told us yesterday, we could have immediately thanked the gods for their kindness!" My father began brewing sake and carving a prayer stick. When he had finished, he offered them to the god of the alder tree, the god of the swamp ash tree and the god of the white wireworm and thanked them, by performing a sacred ceremony with great care.

God, without me ever noticing, prompted me to do battle with this bear and then having put my life in danger, inspired me to beg for their divine help. In this way the gods did a perfect job—using me to slay the bear.

And after that I was married to a most beautiful bride, was blessed with many children and lived happily ever after.

And thus spoke one Ainu.

An altar made for the *Iomante* bear festival.

The u-e-peker—"The Two-Headed Bear" reveals much about the Ainu's concept of God with everything in nature being a god and treated as sacred. Many gods appear in "The Two-Headed Bear" story including the god of the alder tree, the god of the swamp ash tree and the god of the white wireworm. Mountains, rivers, springs, trees, animals and fish, and all of nature are revered and respected as gods. Useful things are also considered to be gods, and each time after the use of tools and materials, thanks is given to the gods with a prayer stick and sake offering.

But if an accident happens in the mountains or in a river, that particular god is severely scolded by saying, "You were negligent god, and now look what has happened!" I remember hearing my father scolding the god of the mountains when my brother fell out of a tree saying, "Oh, god of the mountains, your lack of attention has caused a child to fall out of a tree in your garden! Be more careful, and don't let this happen again!"

In the "The Two-Headed Bear" story, the gods are told, "And you—the many gods of this land, how could you stand by and watch this happen without doing anything about this? I am not prepared to allow it!" And later god is even threatened, "If you desert me now and let me die, it is for sure that the awful stench arising from my corpse will rise up to heaven as a mist and trouble you forever!"

The Ainu speak to the gods in this manner because they believe they are on equal terms with the gods and in exchange for taking good care of the gods, they expect the gods to do the same for the Ainu. This is the Ainu idea about God.

A Poem For the River Saru

One day, Kanna Kamuy, the God of Heaven,
Wished to see the Saru River.
Watching the river flow below,
Slowly, slowly, Kanna Kamuy came upstream from the sea.

The banks of the river were lined with beautiful willows.
The river overflowed with salmon,
The sun scorching the backs of those on the surface.
The rocks ripping off the bellies of those at the river bottom.
So full was the river with salmon pushing against one another.

(from a kamuy yukar, a short Ainu epic poem)

Author

Kayano Shigeru (1926 ~) born and raised with Ainu as his mother tongue, in Nibutani, Southeastern Hokkaido, personally witnessed the almost systematic destruction of the whole Ainu way of life. Since 1953, he has devoted himself to the preservation and use of the Ainu language and culture by both collecting Ainu folk objects and folktales and founding or helping to found fourteen Ainu language schools. Mr. Kayano has published numerous books of Ainu folktales and culture, two of which have been translated into English: *The Romance of the Bear Gods: Ainu Folktales* (Taishukan 1985) and *Our Land Was a Forest— An Ainu Memoir* (Westview Press 1994). He has received various prestigious awards including the Kikuchi Kan Literary Award (1975), the Yoshikawa Eiji Literary Award (1989), and the Hokkaido Cultural Award (1993).

In 1988, during the now infamous Nibutani Dam forced expropriation of sacred Ainu land by the Japanese government he is reputed to have said: *"We the Ainu People have no recollection of ever having sold or lent this big island of Hokkaido to Japan. If the Japanese government says that we have sold it to them, let them show us the documents or call forth the witnesses. If they say we have lent it to them, let them show us the terms of the agreement..."* In saying this, the Ainu elder and statesman is acknowledged to have spoken on behalf of the plight of all aboriginal peoples across the world. In 1994 Mr. Kayano was also the first Ainu in history to ever become a member of the Japanese parliament. He lives in Nibutani, Hokkaido and is currently the director of the Kayano Shigeru Ainu Memorial Museum.

Illustrator

Iijima Shunichi was born in Hokkaido in 1922. He was a woodblock and oil painting artist and worked on numerous woodblock prints depicting the historical relations of the Ainu and the Japanese. Among his works are *The Ainu Series 1,2 and 3.* His work has been displayed in numerous international exhibits.

Author of Preface

David T. Suzuki, a third generation Japanese Canadian, is an award-winning scientist, environmentalist and broadcaster. He is well known as the host of many popular science television series such as *The Nature of Things, A Planet for the Taking, The Secret of Life, The Brain,* and *The Sacred Balance.* An internationally respected geneticist, Dr. Suzuki was a full Professor at the University of British Columbia in Vancouver until his retirement and now is professor emeritus with UBC's Sustainable Development Research Institute. He has won numerous awards for his works including a UNESCO prize for science, a United Nations Environment Program medal, and the Order of Canada. For his work in support of Canada's First Nations people, he has received many tributes and has been honored with five names and formal adoption by two tribes. The author and co-author of more than thirty books, including *Wisdom of the Elders* (Stoddart), Dr. Suzuki is recognized as a world leader in sustainable ecology and he is Chairperson of the David Suzuki Foundation (http://www.davidsuzuki.org/).

Translators

Peter Howlett was born and raised in Hokkaido. He is currently an EFL teacher at Hakodate La Salle Jr. and Sr. High Schools. He is also the chairperson of the Southern Hokkaido Natural Energy Project.

Richard McNamara lives in Aso Kuju National Park, Kyushu with his wife and family. Peter and Richard have also translated the well-loved Guri and Gura and Little Daruma children's books, as well as *Sushi for Kids,* all from Tuttle Publishing.

The translators wish to thank the following fellow Project U-e-peker members for their assistance; Owaki Noriyoshi, Shimizu Yuji, Rob Witmer, Deborah Davidson, Nomura Kenji, and Sugiyama Joji, along with special thanks to Oiwa Keibo.

Published by Periplus Editions (HK) Ltd, with editorial offices at 153 Milk Street, Boston, Massachusetts 02109 and 130 Joo Seng Road, #06-01/03 Singapore 368357.

Text © Kayano Shigeru, 1989
Illustrations © Iijima Shunichi, 1989
First published in 1989 by Fukuinkan Shoten Publishers, Inc., Tokyo, Japan
First Tuttle edition, 2004
All rights reserved. No part of this publication may be reproduced, stored in a retrieval system or transmitted in any form or by any means, electronic, mechanical, photocopying, recording or otherwise without prior permission of the publisher.

LCC No: 2003110006
ISBN 0-8048-3511-X
ISBN 4-8053-0708-0 (for sale in Japan)

Printed in Singapore
First printing, 2004

09 08 07 06 05 04
6 5 4 3 2 1

Distributed by:

Japan:
Tuttle Publishing, Yaekari Building, 3F 5-4-12 Osaki, Shinagawa-ku, Tokyo 141-0032
Tel: (03) 5437 0171, Fax: (03) 5437 0755
Email: tuttle-sales@gol.com

North America, Latin America & Europe:
Tuttle Publishing, 364 Innovation Drive
North Clarendon, VT 05759-9436
Tel: (802) 773 8930, Fax: (802) 773 6993
Email: info@tuttlepublishing.com

Asia Pacific:
Berkeley Books Pte Ltd
130 Joo Seng Road #06-01, Singapore 368357
Tel: (65) 6280 1330, Fax: (65) 6280 6290
Email: inquiries@periplus.com.sg

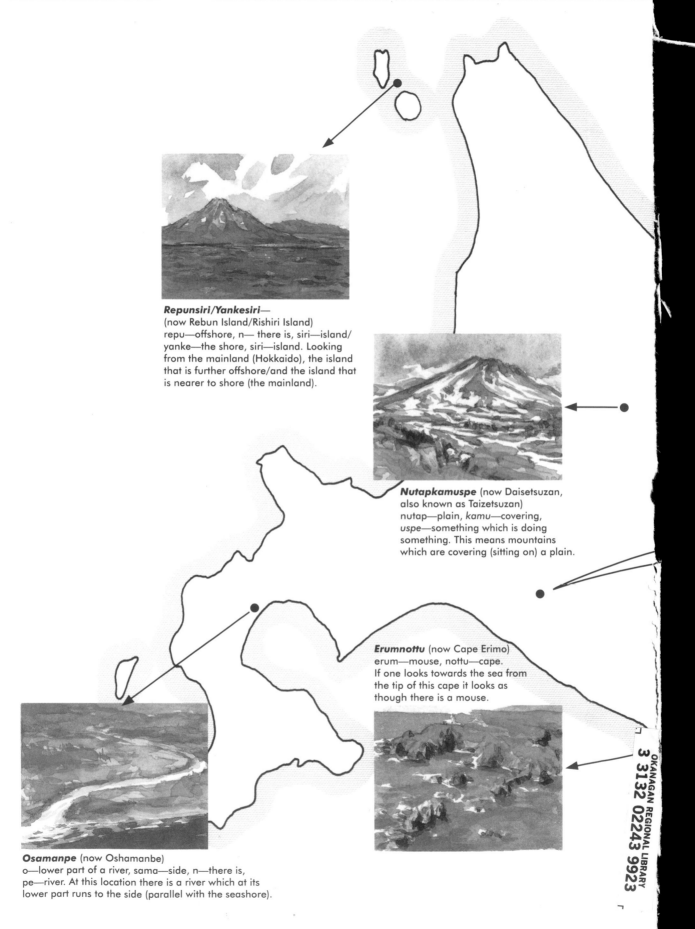

Repunsiri/Yankesiri—
(now Rebun Island/Rishiri Island)
repu—offshore, n— there is, siri—island/
yanke—the shore, siri—island. Looking
from the mainland (Hokkaido), the island
that is further offshore/and the island that
is nearer to shore (the mainland).

Nutapkamuspe (now Daisetsuzan,
also known as Taizetsuzan)
nutap—plain, kamu—covering,
uspe—something which is doing
something. This means mountains
which are covering (sitting on) a plain.

Erumnottu (now Cape Erimo)
erum—mouse, nottu—cape.
If one looks towards the sea from
the tip of this cape it looks as
though there is a mouse.

Osamanpe (now Oshamanbe)
o—lower part of a river, sama—side, n—there is,
pe—river. At this location there is a river which at its
lower part runs to the side (parallel with the seashore).

OKANAGAN REGIONAL LIBRARY
3 3132 02243 9923